Let Me FiNiSH!

by Minh Lê

illustrated by Isabel Roxas

Disney • HYPERION

LOS ANGELES   NEW YORK

First Edition, June 2016 • 10 9 8 7 6 5 4 3 2 1 • FAC-029191-16046

Printed in Malaysia

Library of Congress Cataloging-in-Publication Data
Lê, Minh
Let me finish! / by Minh Lê ; illustrated by Isabel Roxas.—First edition.
pages cm
Summary: "A young boy wants to read his favorite books
without interruption, but the creatures around him keep spoiling
the ending!"—Provided by publisher.
ISBN 978-1-4847-2173-5—ISBN 1-4847-2173-X
[1. Books and reading—Fiction. 2. Animals—Fiction. 3. Humorous stories.]
I. Roxas, Isabel, illustrator. II. Title.
PZ7.1.L39Le 2016
[E—dc23   2015011775

Reinforced binding

Visit www.DisneyBooks.com

For my parents from the start,
and for Aimée till the end
—M.L.

For all the voracious readers of the world
who believe that to love a book is to share it.
And to those who love them anyway.
—I.R.

Ahhhh . . . nothing like a quiet spot and a new book.

Hey, I was just getting started, and you've already ruined the ending! Next time, please let me finish.

Found it!

I've been meaning to
read this one forever.

Now to find a peaceful spot
where I won't be disturbed.

But then they saved the poor thing from the well!
What a surprise ending!
Grandma to the rescue!
OH NO!

Not **again**.

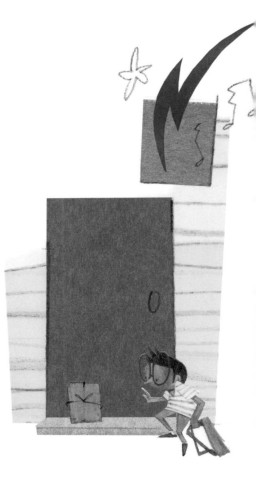

Hmm,
what have we here?

Yes! I've been waiting all
year for this book.

No one better spoil this one for me.

Here we go. I can't wait to dive in.

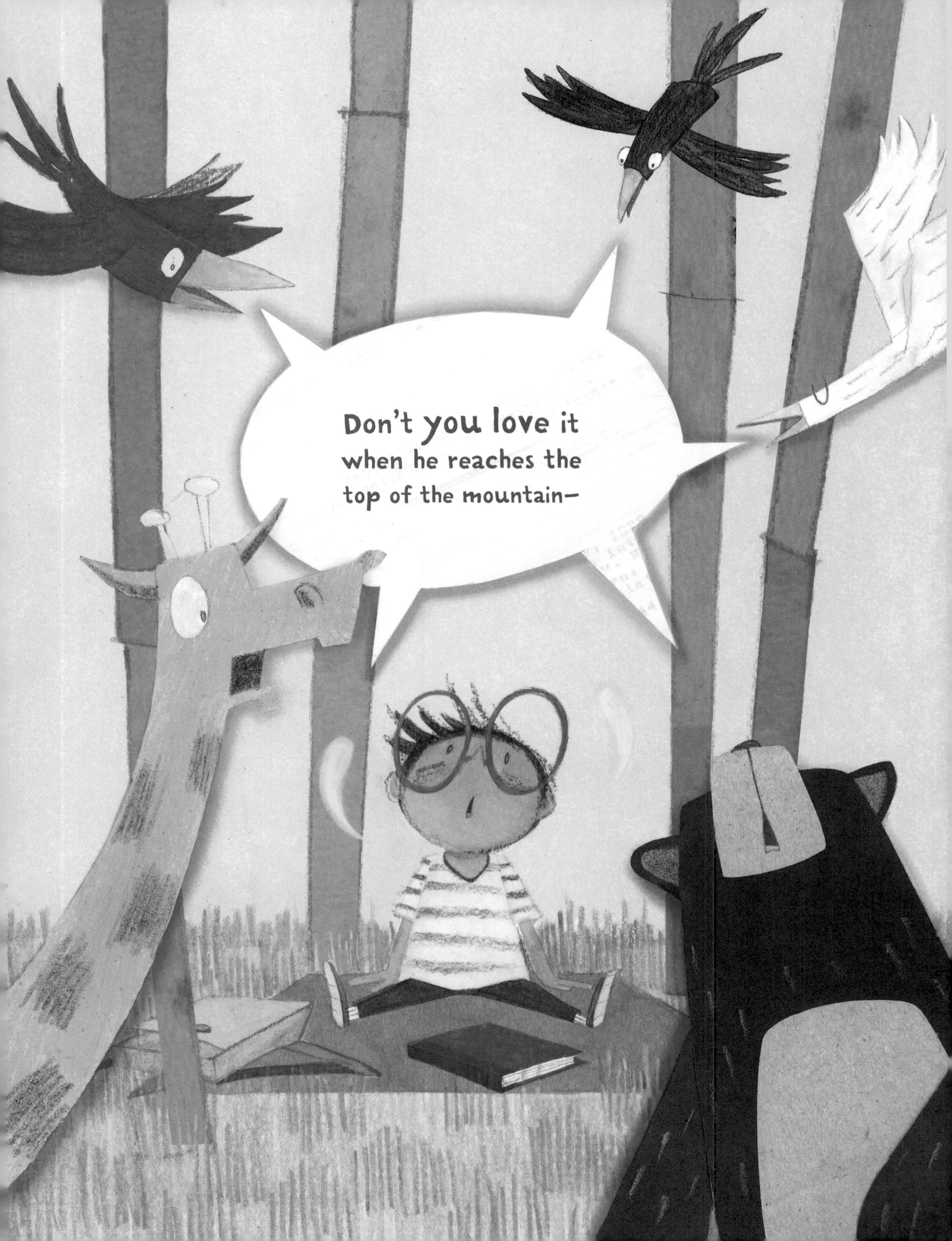
Don't you love it when he reaches the top of the mountain–

No!

Not this time!

This time I'm making it to the end!

JUST LET ME FINISH!

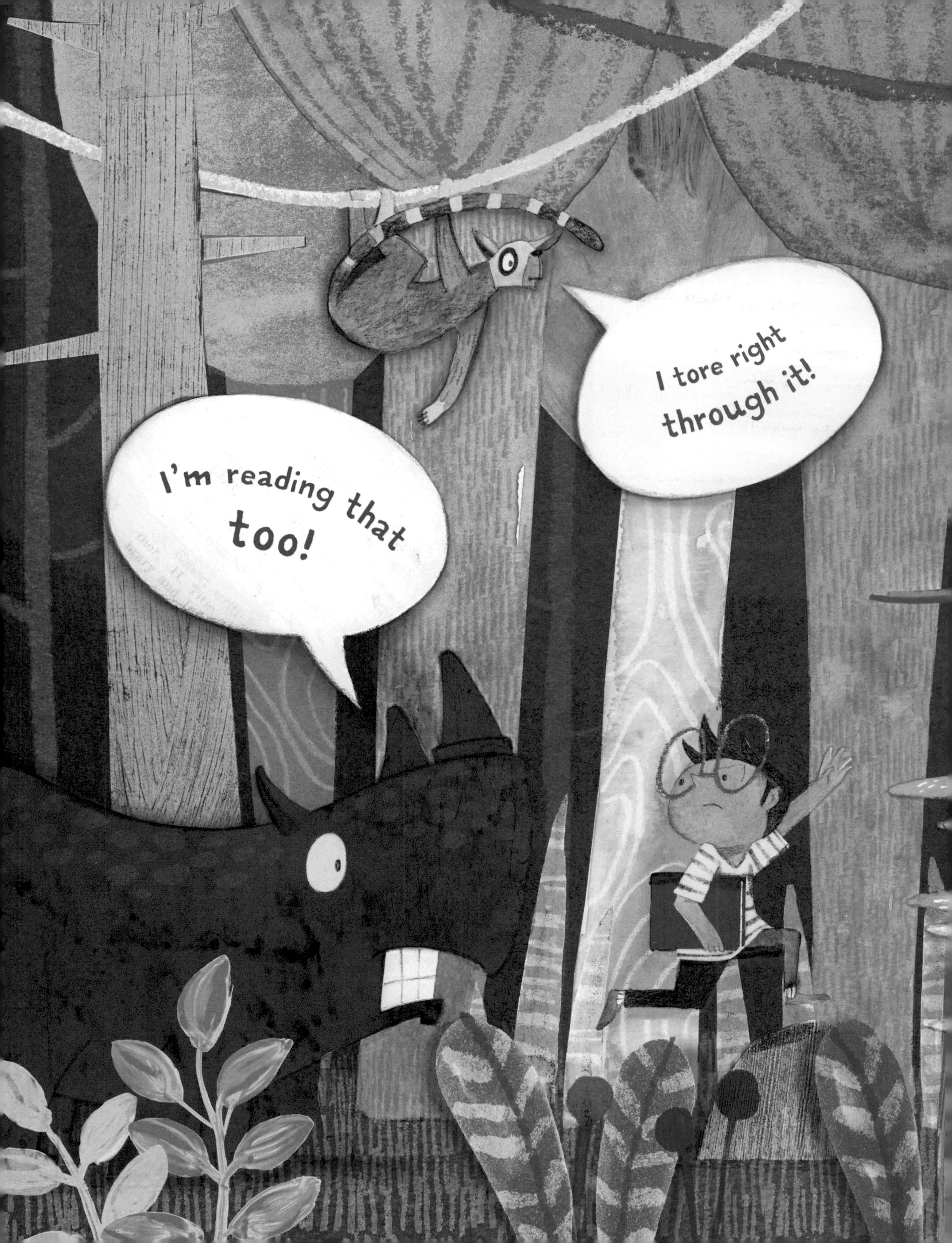
I tore right through it!
I'm reading that too!

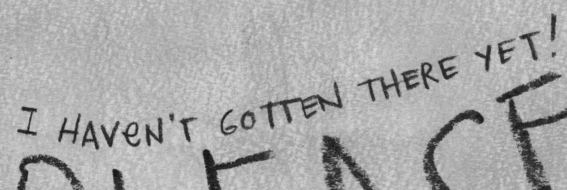

Watch out for
the dinosaur at the—

LA-LA-LA!!!
I can't hear you!

LA-LA-LA!!!
I'm begging you!

Finally, all alone.

I think I just did. . . .

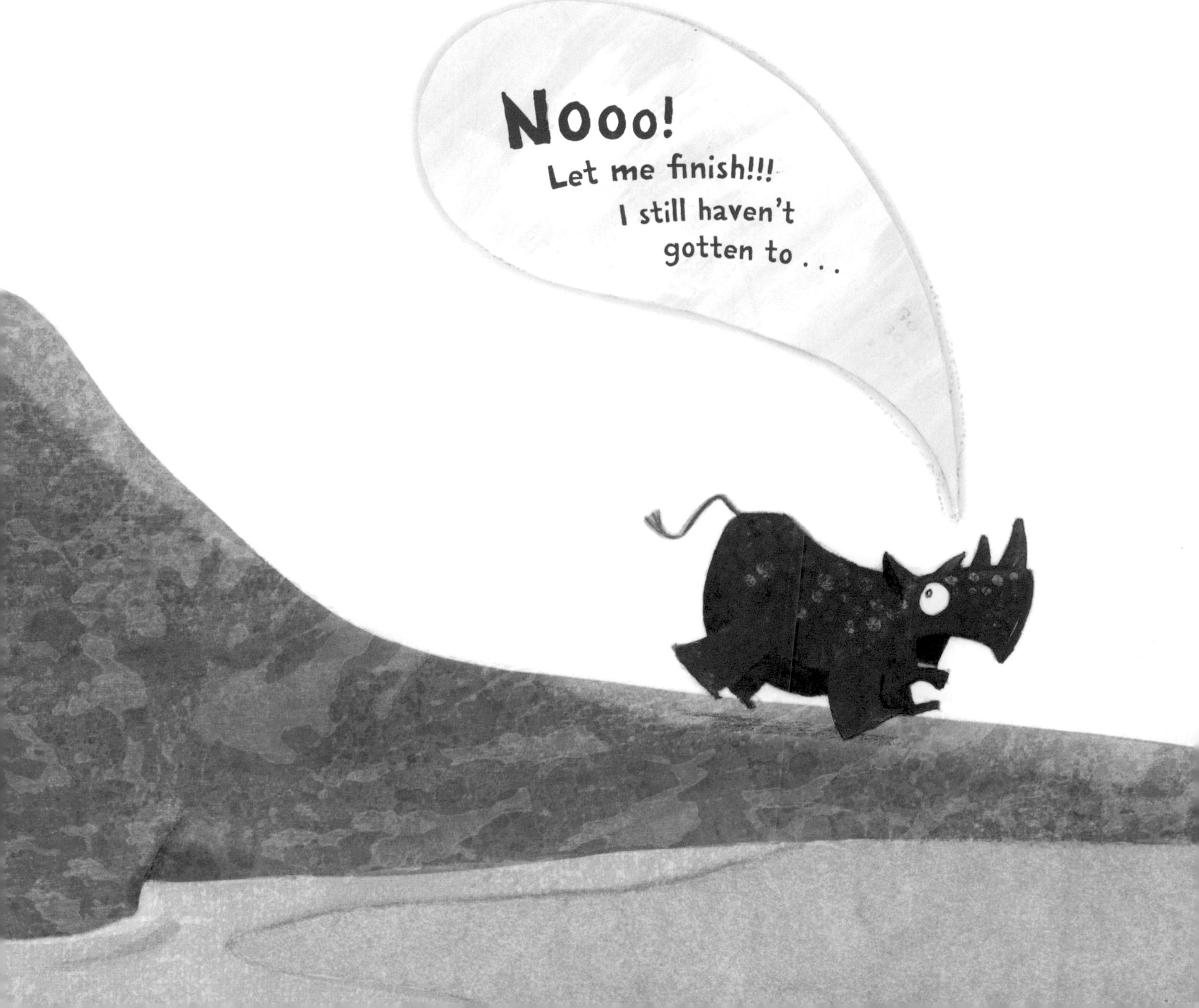
Nooo!
Let me finish!!!
I still haven't
gotten to . . .

The End.